Dear Parent:

Congratulations! Your child is taking the first steps on an exciting journey. The destination? Independent reading!

STEP INTO READING® will help your child get there. The program offers five steps to reading success. Each step includes fun stories and colorful art. There are also Step into Reading Sticker Books, Step into Reading Math Readers, Step into Reading Phonics Readers, Step into Reading Write-In Readers, and Step into Reading Phonics Boxed Sets—a complete literacy program with something for every child.

Learning to Read, Step by Step!

Ready to Read   Preschool–Kindergarten
• big type and easy words • rhyme and rhythm • picture clues
For children who know the alphabet and are eager to begin reading.

Reading with Help   Preschool–Grade 1
• basic vocabulary • short sentences • simple stories
For children who recognize familiar words and sound out new words with help.

Reading on Your Own   Grades 1–3
• engaging characters • easy-to-follow plots • popular topics
For children who are ready to read on their own.

Reading Paragraphs   Grades 2–3
• challenging vocabulary • short paragraphs • exciting stories
For newly independent readers who read simple sentences with confidence.

Ready for Chapters   Grades 2–4
• chapters • longer paragraphs • full-color art
For children who want to take the plunge into chapter books but still like colorful pictures.

STEP INTO READING® is designed to give every child a successful reading experience. The grade levels are only guides. Children can progress through the steps at their own speed, developing confidence in their reading, no matter what their grade.

Remember, a lifetime love of reading starts with a single step!

Special thanks to Diane Reichenberger, Cindy Ledermann, Ann McNeill, Kim Culmone, Emily Kelly, Sharon Woloszyk, Carla Alford, Rita Lichtwardt, Kathy Berry, Rob Hudnut, David Wiebe, Shelley Dvi-Vardhana, Gabrielle Miles, Technicolor, and Walter P. Martishius.

Published in the United States by Random House Children's Books, a division of Random House, Inc., 1745 Broadway, New York, NY 10019, and in Canada by Random House of Canada Limited, Toronto.

Step into Reading, Random House, and the Random House colophon are registered trademarks of Random House, Inc.

Visit us on the Web!
StepIntoReading.com
randomhouse.com/kids

Educators and librarians, for a variety of teaching tools, visit us at RHTeachersLibrarians.com

ISBN 978-0-307-98115-8 (trade) — ISBN 978-0-307-98116-5 (lib. bdg.)

Printed in the United States of America   10 9 8 7 6

Ballet Dreams

Adapted by Kristen L. Depken
Based on the original screenplay by Alison Taylor
Illustrated by Ulkutay Design Group

Random House 🏠 New York

Kristyn is a ballerina.

She wants

to be a ballet star.

Tara is
the ballet school's
star dancer.
She gets to be the lead
in all the shows.

It is Kristyn's turn
to dance.
She does not follow
the dance steps.
She dances
her own way.
She tears her shoes.

Kristyn's friend Hailey
takes her
to the costume shop.
Kristyn gets
new pink shoes.

Kristyn puts
the shoes on.
They shimmer.

Kristyn's hair
changes color!
Her dress turns blue.
The shoes sparkle!

They take

Kristyn and Hailey

to a magic ballet world!

Kristyn and Hailey are
in a ballet story.
Kristyn is the lead!

It is not just a show.
The ballet is real!

An evil Snow Queen
arrives.

She is mad.

Kristyn and Hailey
should not be
in this ballet.
They run and hide.

Kristyn's hair and dress
change again!
She and Hailey are
in a new ballet story.
Kristyn gets a crown.
She is now the
Swan Queen.

Kristyn dances
with a prince.
He falls in love.

A bad wizard turns
Kristyn and Hailey
into swans!
He wants the prince
to marry his daughter.

Kristyn and Hailey
fly to the palace.
They will stop the
wizard.

The bad wizard

tricks the prince.

The prince dances
with the wizard's
daughter.
She looks like
the Swan Queen.

Kristyn and Hailey

stop the dance.

They break the spell!

Kristyn dances
with the prince.

The Snow Queen

is angry.

Kristyn is changing

the ballet story again.

The Snow Queen

takes Hailey away!

Kristyn rushes
to the ice palace.
The Snow Queen
puts a spell on her.
Kristyn dances.
Her dance breaks
the spell.
The Snow Queen melts!

Hailey is free!

She thanks Kristyn.

Kristyn takes

off the pink shoes.

She and Hailey

go home.

Kristyn dances
in the big show.
She dances
her own steps.
It is magical!
The audience cheers.
They love her!

Kristyn did not dance
like Tara.

She danced like herself!

The girls curtsy.

They are both
ballet stars now!